KEE

A
ZODIUS
NOVELLA

New York Times Bestselling Author

LISA RENEE JONES

GLOSSARY

Area 51—Another name used for Groom Lake.

Blood Exchange—A part of the lifebond process done by choice, after the lifebond mark appears on the female's neck. This completes the female's transformation to GTECH and links the two lifebonds in life and death. (See Lifebond Process.)

Bar-1—A brainwashing program that isolates brain neurons and allows brainwashing to occur. It will only work on females, not on males.

Dreamland—Though Groom Lake/Area 51 is often called Dreamland, in The Renegades series, Dreamland is the fictional military facility opened eighty miles from Area 51 by General Powell to take a stand against the Zodius who overran Area 51.

Green Hornet—Special bullet that is so powerful it not only shreds human muscle and bone, it permeates the thin bodysuit armor that the GTECHs—both Zodius and Renegades—wear when no other bullet can do so.

Groom Lake—Also known as Area 51, this is the military base where the Project Zodius experiments with alien DNA took place, which was later taken over by the Zodius rebels.

GTECH—The Super Soldiers who were created under Project Zodius and who divided into two groups—Zodius and Renegades. GTECHs are stronger, faster, and more agile than humans; they heal rapidly and have low fatality rates. They can wind-walk. Over time, many are developing special gifts unique to them, such as telepathy, ability to communicate with animals, and more.

GTECH Body Armor—A thin bodysuit that fits like a second skin. Extremely light and flexible. The material is made from alien technology recovered from a 1950s crash site. Until the Green Hornets were created, no standard issue ammunition could penetrate the suits.

GTECH Serum—The serum created from alien DNA that was gathered at a crash site in the 1950s and then used to create the GTECHs. The original sample was destroyed. Since the alien DNA will not allow itself to be duplicated, there can be no new serum created without new scientific discoveries. The remaining serum disappeared the day Area 51/Groom Lake was taken over by the GTECH Rebels known as Zodius Soldiers. The GTECH serum cannot be created from GTECH DNA. This has been tried and failed.

Lifebond Mark—A double circle resembling a tattoo appears on the back of the female's neck after the first sexual encounter with a GTECH, but only the female meant to be that GTECH's Lifebond. After the mark appears, the female feels a tingling sensation whenever the male Lifebond first approaches.

Lifebond Process—A Lifebond is a male and female who are bonded physically for life and death. If one dies, so does the other. This bond allows the GTECH male to reproduce, and it offers the females the same physical skills as their male Lifebond. The lifebond mark, a double circle resembling a tattoo, appears on the back of the female's neck after the first sexual encounter. A blood exchange is required to complete the physical transformation of the female to GTECH, if the couple makes that decision. There is physical pain and illness for the female during conversion.

Neonopolis—The Las Vegas satellite location for the Renegades, covertly located in the basement of the Neonopolis entertainment complex off Las Vegas Avenue.

PMI or "Private Military Intelligence"—A company run by General Powell, the officer who created Project Zodius. PMI is used as a cover for top-secret military projects that the government doesn't want to officially show on the books.

Project Zodius—Code name for the government's top-secret operation—two hundred Special Operations soldiers who were assigned to Groom Lake (Area 51) and injected with what they believed to be immunizations, but which was, in fact, alien DNA.

Red Dart—A red crystal found at the same UFO 1950s crash site where the GTECH DNA was discovered. The crystal creates a red laser beam that enters the bloodstream and creates a permanent tracking beacon that is sensitive to sound waves. These sound waves can also be used for torture and control of the GTECHs. Thus far, U.S. military attempts to use Red Dart have been fatal.

Renegade Soldier—A GTECH who protects humanity and stands against the rebels known as "Zodius." The Renegades are led by Adam Rain's twin brother, Caleb Rain.

Shield—A mental barrier that a GTECH uses to block their psychic residue from being traceable by Trackers.

Stardust—An alien substance that is undetectable in human testing and causes brain aneurisms.

Sunrise City—The main Renegades facility, an advanced, underground city located in Nevada's Sunrise Mountain Range.

Trackers—These are GTECHs with the special ability to track the psychic residue of another GTECH or a human female who's been intimate with another GTECH. If a female possesses this residue, then only that female's Lifebond can shield her from a Tracker.

Wardens—An all-female group of women who have joined to stop the abductions of other women by the Zodius.

Wind-walking—The ability to fade into the wind, like mist into the air, and invisibly travel far distances at rapid speed.

X2 Gene—A gene that appears in some, but not all, of the GTECHs by the fifteenth month after injection of the GTECH serum.

Zodius City—Still known as the top-secret U.S. military facility often called Area 51 or Groom Lake, located in Nevada, it was taken over by the rebel GTECHs led by Adam Rain. This facility is both above and beneath ground level.

Zodius Soldier—A rebel GTECH soldier who follows Adam Rain, the leader of the rebel movement. Adam intends to take over the world.

PROLOGUE

It was near midnight on a hot Vegas summer night as Kelvin 'Kel' Smith rode his Ninja 650 motorcycle down the street where Sonia lived. He could almost smell her rose-scented honey-colored hair, could almost taste the richness of her kisses. Seeing her again was what had kept him going on a three-month-long mission from absolute hell. She didn't know he was home any more than she knew he'd spent these months in a jungle as infested with snakes as it had been with terrorists. He wasn't supposed to be home, but when a helicopter had shown up and handed him new orders twenty-four hours before, he wasn't about to argue. He was home, or he would be when he had Sonia in his arms again.

He'd barely stopped the bike in her driveway before he was off and heading for the door, a ring burning a hole in his jeans pocket. Her birthday was in two days and it was going to kill him to wait to give it to her until then.

He'd taken one step onto the porch when the door flew open.

"Kel!"

The next thing he knew he had the sexiest, sweetest woman in all of Vegas in his arms and she was wearing nothing but one of his army green t-shirts. "How can you be here? You weren't supposed to be home for months."

"Change of orders," he said, slanting his mouth over hers with a hunger he didn't even begin to sate. "I've missed the hell out of you." He lifted her and carried her into the house, kicking the door shut and not stopping until he was in the bedroom.

He went down on the bed, framing her body with his, kissing her, needing her.

"Your hair is longer," she said, stroking her fingers through his chin-length dark brown hair." She gave him a playful smile. "It's sexy."

"In that case, I'll do my best to keep it this way." He leaned in to kiss her again.

She stopped him with a plea. "Tell me you aren't leaving again anytime soon."

"I'm being moved to a special unit at Area 51," he said. "I won't know what that means until next week." He stroked her hair from her face. "How are your nightmares, baby? I've been worried sick about you."

She laughed without humor. "You've been worried about me. You don't know worry until the person you love is off on a mission trying to save lives and willing to give up their own to do it. I'm proud of you, Kel, but it's hard when you're gone."

"I know, baby. Maybe this new base assignment will mean more time at home. You didn't answer me about the nightmares. Are you still having them?"

"Not for over a month," she said, her fingers caressing under his shirt, heating his skin. "I think...maybe they've ended. I don't know but I don't want to talk right now. I just want you." She wrapped her arms around him and pressed those soft, womanly curves against him, and he quickly forgot all about her nightmares, and his for that matter.

In fact, he was pretty sure he'd died and gone to heaven, and she was the angel standing between him and hell.

CHAPTER ONE

Three years later...

Kel materialized through an open window from inside a strand of wind, and stood in the center of a small Vegas warehouse not far from the strip. While the location wasn't his final destination and traveling inside the wind was a common skill that the GTECH Super Soldiers created in an Area 51 experiment possessed, it wasn't exactly something the public needed to know about. The last thing Kel and his team, the Renegades, needed was a bunch of Van Helsing wannabe hunters calling them monsters, and trying to kill them all off. Especially when the Renegades were all that stood between man and the Zodius, the GTECH rebels, who really were worthy of the title 'monsters'.

Damion Browne, one of his fellow Renegades, appeared by his side.

"Took you long enough, Mr. America," Kel jibed, using the nickname they'd all given Damion, because he was all about morality and restoring the honor of the army and his country. Kel, well, he didn't have a lot of faith in that happening, not after their special forces unit had been told they were getting immunizations, when they were really given experimental DNA. But hell, as long as he didn't have to don any red, white, and blue leotard, he was willing to play superhero, and see where it landed them. Kel glanced at his watch. "You're a full ten seconds behind on the landing. Getting slow in your old age. Oh, right. We don't age anymore, so you're just slow."

"I wasn't aware it was a race," Damion commented dryly.

"Confucius say 'Life's always a race," Kel said, "then you die'." They started walking toward an elevator.

Damion flipped him an incredulous look. "Confucius did not say that."

"No," Kel agreed, "but my fortune cookie last night did."

They stepped into the elevator that would lead them to a tunnel beneath the building next door, a huge entertainment complex that drew many a Vegas tourist. They were dressed to blend with the crowd, both in jeans, t-shirt and boots, his with an Aerosmith logo, Damion's a basic black. Kel pulled off the civilian routine pretty darn well with his long brown hair, and his arms and a good portion of his body well inked with tats. Damion, not so much. He was army through and through, from his short military cut to the stern expression that might as well be tattooed on his face. But they weren't there for fun and cotton candy. Roasted peanuts might be on the menu later, after they finished up one of those superhero missions they called their life these days.

"Any idea what this is about?" Kel asked as they stepped off the car and entered the underground tunnel.

"Only that Sterling needed you involved," Damion said. "So I assume they need someone's memory wiped."

A handful of the GTECHs involved in the Area 51 experiments had developed unique abilities. Kel's was one that he carried with some weight on his shoulders. The decision to wipe away someone's memory wasn't something to be taken lightly, but there were times when it saved lives.

It didn't take long before they were inside the facility, standing in a small room with rows of monitors across the front wall. Sterling Jeter, the head of the Renegade's inner-city operation, was facing a master panel when they walked in. His spiky blonde hair was in disarray, as if he'd been running his hands through it in frustration.

Sterling rolled his chair around to face them, his eyes, black as coal like all the GTECHs, fixed on Kel and Kel alone. Tension rolled off the other GTECH and Kel didn't miss the fact that Sterling's normal wise-cracking sense of humor was no more present than his lifebond and wife, Becca—who had some pretty amazing powers of her own—and who was usually by his side. "I have something you need to see," Sterling said.

A ridiculous sense of foreboding had every muscle in Kel's body tensing with a feeling that someone close to him was in danger. There was no one close to him. His father had been killed during a terrorist attack overseas while on active duty, when Kel was still a small child. His mother had died five years before that from cancer. His friends were these men, his fellow GTECHs. But there was someone else, someone he tried not to think about because it hurt too much.

Kel leaned against the wall, trying to calm himself when he'd never had that problem in the past. Never. "I'm all eyes and ears," he said with a remarkably steady voice.

"It seems that the Zodius are bound and determined to find a way around the GTECHs inability to reproduce without an exact perfect female match, now rather than later," Sterling continued. "They seem to be stepping up their fertility testing on human women. Five women disappeared this month from this city alone. Turns out that someone called the police station and told them about one of the abductions before it happened. I got tipped off by my inside guy. The call was made from a public line and hung up about ten seconds before it could be traced. It originated from a pay phone downtown and I managed to hack into the camera feed to get a picture of her."

He rolled his chair around and punched a button, bringing an image up on one monitor. Kel forgot to breathe as he focused on the gorgeous female he knew all too well, and yet, never well enough. Sonia. The woman who should have been his wife. Both Sterling and Damion knew that. They also knew why it hadn't happened.

"Holy crap, Kel," Damion said. "How did Sonia know about the abduction?"

Kel wasn't wasting time explaining Sonia seeing premonitions in her dreams when she was mixed up in something far too dangerous. He'd thought the damn things had stopped but apparently, they hadn't. He pushed off the wall. "Who else knows about this?"

"Too many people," Sterling said. "She's in danger. There's buzz on the streets. Adam is after her."

Adam referred to Adam Rain, the leader of the Zodius movement, and the twin brother of the Renegade's leader, Caleb. Adam wouldn't just kill her. He'd use her for his damnable fertility testing, and try to mate her with every GTECH in Zodius Nation.

"Where is she?" he asked, knowing that Sterling wouldn't have brought him here unless he knew exactly where she was.

"Waitressing at the Coyote Ugly bar," he said. "All five of the women who've disappeared were waitresses at various bars. None from this one. I'm guessing she thinks that's about to change."

From a safe job as a research assistant at a law office to working at the Coyote Ugly bar. Kel was not happy with this turn of events. He was already opening the door, heading for the exit.

"I'm going with you," Damion said.

"I need to do this on my own."

"Like I said," Damion repeated. "I'm going with you. You worry about your woman. I'll worry about the Zodius."

Only Sonia wasn't his woman. Not anymore. She thought he was dead.

KEL

CHAPTER TWO

Loud music thrummed through the bar as Sonia Carmichael delivered drinks to a table and endured the hot male stares of her customers, wondering if one, or all of them, could be responsible for the disappearance of so many women. She wished her dreams had given her faces to go with the men in fatigues kidnapping women. The thought made her all the more thankful that the cowboy boots she wore allowed her a place to hide her gun. It wasn't like the tiny blue-jean shorts and half shirt would hold much. She was even more thankful that she'd come inches from a career in law enforcement, before becoming a research assistant, and knew how to use it. When you had nightmares like hers, a gun felt necessary, and since she'd stopped suppressing the dreams, now that she owned them, she regretted not following in her father's FBI footsteps. He wouldn't have let fear stop him any more than Kel had, and neither of them would have let her be afraid. But they weren't alive, and she had to do this. They both died protecting innocent lives and she wouldn't dishonor them by not doing so herself.

Sonia followed a pretty blonde named Carrie toward the bar. She was a college student working for her living, and the star of one of the nightmares she could never escape. For a week now, Sonia had kept Carrie close, befriended her, trying to protect her. She didn't know how quickly the dream would come true, only that it would and she couldn't sit back and do nothing. Her dreams, her nightmares, always came true.

"I'm off in ten," Carrie said. "You in for the night?"

"You're off early tonight? I thought you always worked late on Fridays?"

"I do but tomorrow's my birthday and my boyfriend is taking me out for the day." Her eyes lit up. "I think he's going to propose."

"Oh my gosh!" Sonia exclaimed and hugged Carrie. "That's fabulous." But her stomach knotted at the prospect of Carrie never seeing that happen. She wasn't going to let that happen. Even if she had to guard her every step of the way. "I'm off early tonight, too. Why don't we go for cake somewhere?"

"I'd love that," Carrie said. "I'm parked at the side of the building in the employee lot. You?"

"Same," Sonia said, "See you there."

Carrie grabbed two drinks the bartender had set on the counter and took off. Sonia went in search of the manager to claim an emergency and to try to keep this job, in case she needed it. She inhaled. Actually, maybe she needed to somehow make Carrie lose her job. It was a horrible thing to do but Sonia's dream had directly linked Carrie's kidnapping to this place. It was something to consider after tonight. Tonight she just needed to get Carrie home safely.

<hr>

Just past midnight, Sonia and Carrie exited the side door of the building, both having donned sweatshirts. Overhead lights cast a soft glow on the desolate parking lot. Everyone else was inside, working or having fun. Sonia's oversized purse hung on her shoulder, her hand stuffed inside, wrapped around the gun she'd relocated for easier access.

"How about Joe's bakery?" Carrie asked. "It's a five-minute drive and they're open until two."

"Sounds like a plan to me," Sonia said. Anything to get Carrie in her car and away from here.

They both headed to their vehicles when the wind suddenly picked up. Sonia had no idea what made her react except instinct. She grabbed Carrie and pulled her close, at the same time pulling out her gun. Suddenly, out of nowhere, three men in black fatigues appeared in front of them. It was as if they had come from the air or wind. Carrie screeched and clung to Sonia.

One of the men grabbed Carrie's arm. Sonia fired the gun, hoping it would not only wound their attackers, but get them attention and help. The man let go of Carrie, looking more shocked than injured, which meant he had to be wearing a vest. The other two men laughed which Sonia was pretty sure meant they were in trouble. With no other options, Sonia continued to pull the trigger, knowing enough about vests to know the bullets still hurt.

The wind lifted again. Two more men appeared, on Sonia's left and right, and she had a dim awareness of them wearing jeans, not fatigues like the others, like the men in her nightmares.

The three men in fatigues turned to the newcomers in obvious confrontation, and Sonia leaned into Carrie, and whispered, "Run!" Together they and rushed for the door. Sonia could hear a battle starting behind them – grunts and growls.

Sonia and Carrie were all but at the door to the club when a man appeared out of nowhere. They turned to the run the other way and another man appeared from nowhere. Just materialized as if by magic. Only, Sonia gasped at the familiar face.

"Damion?" She stared in shock at an old army buddy of Kel's.

"Yes," he said. "And do what I say and everything is going to be okay." He reached for Carrie.

"Sonia?" Carrie asked, but Sonia never got to answer. Damion shoved a needle in Carrie's arm and she passed out.

Sonia didn't have time to react to Damion's unexpected action. She had a sudden awareness of someone at her back and whirled around to land against a hard body. She was instantly certain she was dreaming. The scent of him, and the feel of him, sent a rush of memories through her. It couldn't be who she thought it was. The world started to spin as her chin lifted and she brought the man into view.

"Kel?" she gasped, a moment before he stuck a needle into her arm and everything went black.

CHAPTER THREE

Sonia came awake with a gasp and sat up in a strange bed. Her gaze flew around the room, what looked like a studio apartment with a leather couch and chair directly in front of her and a dining room to the right.

"You're safe," came the familiar male voice that she knew couldn't be real.

She turned slowly and went to her knees to bring the black leather chair sitting in the corner by the bed into her view. And there he sat, the man she'd loved, the man she'd lost. His hair was longer now, loose around his shoulders, his eyes the same iridescent crystal blue.

"I'm dreaming again," she whispered, her heart beating wildly in her chest. He couldn't be here.

"You're not dreaming," he said. "It's me."

She didn't go to him. She wanted to, but she was afraid the dream would shift and he'd be gone. He seemed as if he was afraid to move, too. "You aren't real."

He nodded. "I'm real."

"Kel?"

"Yeah baby, it's me."

She was off the bed and in his embrace in a flash, wrapping her arms around him, feeling his heat sink in through her thin shirt. "I can't believe it. I can't believe you're here. You're real. You're really here." He kissed her and it was heaven, spicy and male, and so very Kel, so real, so perfect. "How? How is this possible?" She couldn't stop touching him, trying to prove to herself he was flesh and blood.

"It's complicated," he whispered, his mouth caressing hers, holding her close, like he thought she might escape. "God, I missed you."

She pulled back, tracking the lines of his face. Kel. Kel was alive. After nearly three years of believing he was dead. "Are you sure this isn't a dream?"

"It feels like one to me," he murmured, his lips brushing her neck, her ear. "I didn't think I'd ever hold you like this again."

A shiver of pure heat rushed down her spine, the kind of need no one but Kel could create. "Me either," she said, kissing him, caressing his cheek. She was sitting across his lap now, and all she wanted to do was get lost in the man she'd lost and now found, but memories rushed over her of their free will, and Carrie's screeches of fear ripped through her mind. "You're sure my friend from the bar is safe?"

"Absolutely."

"The men, they came out of nowhere. There was wind and then they were there. And you too. I'm confused. I don't understand what happened back there at the bar. I don't understand how you're alive or how I'm here and why did you put me to sleep?"

"We're at one of the top-secret facilities where my special ops team operates," he said. "I had to put you to sleep. It's protocol."

Her stomach knotted. Something wasn't right. "Kel, what's going on?"

He maneuvered so that she sat in the chair and he knelt in front of her. "Sonia, I...it's not easy to explain. I..." He lowered his head and a wave of emotion rolled off of him.

Her hand stroked his hair. "What is it?" she asked gently, certain whatever he'd been through must have been horrific, since everyone had believed he was dead.

When he lifted his head, his expression was etched with torment. "I didn't want this for you, Sonia. I didn't want you in danger. I didn't want you to give up everything you knew to live in a world that is this messed up. But you got the wrong people's attention when you made that phone call about the missing woman, and now, now everything has changed."

She stiffened, dread pooling in her stomach. "What are you saying? Oh, God. No. I don't believe this. You faked your death to get me out of your life, didn't you?"

"It's not like that, Sonia-"

Confirmation hit her hard. She shoved away from him and stood up, stepping around him and backed away. "Then how it is? You're alive and clearly everyone but me knew that. Do you have any idea what hell I have lived thinking you were dead?"

He rose to his feet. "Sonia-"

"Did you fake your death for me?" she demanded, every word tight and exact. She was shaking. Tears prickled at the back of her eyes.

"I was trying to protect you."

She hugged herself. Protect her. She didn't even know what to say to that. "Why show yourself to me now?"

"Because I'm no longer the most dangerous person in your life."

"You haven't even been in my life so how could you be dangerous?"

"That's the idea," he said. "I had to stay away. And it killed me. I know you don't understand, but-"

"I understand that you chose for me, which must mean you didn't want me anymore. Why not just break up with me Kel? Why? Why let me mourn you?"

"Leaving you behind killed me, Sonia," he said, his voice raspy with emotion she knew had to be fake. He'd left her. He'd walked away like she was nothing.

"And yet you did."

"You would have chosen me," he said. "I had to choose you."

"By playing dead?"

"Yes," he ground out, drawing out the word. "I chose your safety. You don't understand what happened. I'll explain-"

"You are Special Forces," she said. "I knew the danger. Nothing you can say will change how much you hurt me. And now – now you say I'm in danger so you pull me back into your world by necessity, but not choice?"

"It's not like that," he argued and took a step toward her.

She backed away. "And yet it is. It is."

"They changed me, Sonia," he said, his voice gravely and thick. "They turned me into something I don't even recognize."

She hugged herself, not sure how she was holding back the tears, trying to control her shaking. "I don't either, because the man I thought I knew and loved wouldn't have done this to me, to us." She inhaled and let it out. "Can I leave now?"

"It's not that simple."

"Why? What does that mean?"

"It means that you're being hunted by Adam Rain and that's a very dangerous thing to be."

"Caleb's brother?"

"Yes," he said. "Caleb's brother. He's leading a rebel group called the Zodius who took over Area 51 and they intend to take over far more than that."

"What?" she gasped. "Why? When did this happen?"

"The immunizations they were giving us at Area 51 weren't immunizations at all. They were experimental DNA that changed us. We aren't...human. Not fully anymore."

She was stunned. "What does that mean? What kind of DNA?"

"The rumors of a ship that the government recovered in New Mexico were true," he said. "And with it they acquired some unique DNA. After years of study, they finally decided to see if they could create what you might call a 'super soldier' while the government calls them GTECHs."

She gaped in total disbelief. "Oh my God. And they didn't tell you what they were doing?"

His lips thinned. "No. They didn't tell us. The change took months to occur. That's why I didn't initially pull away from you. I simply had no idea what I was or what had happened. Once I knew, I was afraid of what I was becoming. For all I knew I might become a monster that would hurt you, or worse, kill you. Much later, Adam decided the GTECHs were evolution and overthrew Area 51 and created what he calls Zodius Nation."

"Zodius?"

"Project Zodius was the name of the experimental program the Army undertook to make us," he explained before going on. "Caleb organized the Renegades, an opposing force to the Zodius, and I knew I'd made the right decision. Anyone a Renegade loves is a weapon Adam would use against us. Adam had met you. Had I not ended what was between us long before he became the monster he is now, you would have been a target. Now, unfortunately, you are anyway. He might not know you have a special gift, but he thinks you have an insider telling you his plans to kidnap women. He won't stop until he captures you."

She sat on the bed, stunned and unsure she wasn't dreaming. "This seems impossible." Her gaze lifted to his. "Adam is kidnapping the women, then?"

He gave a nod. "The GTECHs are only fertile with one woman. Finding that woman is a mystery and he's conducting dangerous and pretty horrific fertility testing. And if you want to know what that means, ask Sterling's lifebond. She knows firsthand."

"Lifebond? What is a lifebond?"

"The one woman the GTECH is fertile with. Sterling is one of the rare GTECHs who found his."

She inhaled sharply and let it out. "And you?"

"There is no woman for me but you, Sonia. There never has been." He cut his gaze and seemed to grapple for control before slowly shifting his eyes back to hers. "There are things you don't know and I can't tell you right now. I need to leave this room before I do something we will both regret."

The next thing she knew he was stalking past her, clearly headed for the door, and intending to leave.

Would he come back? Would she ever see him again. Sonia pursued him and shackled his arm. "Please don't go. Please. Not when I've just found out you're alive."

"I have to," he said, sounding as if he was in pain. "I don't have control with you and you have no idea the implications of what that means." He ran a rough hand through his hair. "I'll be back. Just...just give me some time. You can't leave the facility, but you can go anywhere inside. I'll send someone to show you around."

"You show me around," she said, regretting how she'd doubted him, how she'd reacted to what he'd told her.

"I can't, Sonia. I just...can't. You don't understand that now but you will. You will." He pulled away and was through the door before she could stop him.

KEL

CHAPTER FOUR

Kel stalked down the hallway toward the lab where he knew he'd find Becca, Sterling's lifebond, someone who could help Sonia in all kinds of ways. Emotion expanded inside him, ready to explode but somehow he clamped down on his feelings. He knew the right thing to do. He knew he had to wipe Sonia's memory as he would the waitress, once they'd arranged a new life for her, someplace safe and far away from the Zodius' reach. Instead, he burned to pull her into his arms and make love to her, to make her his lifebond and bind her to him forever. The bond was no sure thing, and even if it was, it would steal her ability to choose her future. Not this time, not when she had options. And not when the final outcome was her being bound to him in life and in death. She deserved a choice and but he worried it wasn't that simple. The truth of the matter was thought that he wasn't even sure that he really could give her choices. Would her dreams simply recreate whatever he'd erased?

The only person that might be able to answer that was Becca. She had abilities that her transformation to GTECH had given her.

He entered the lab, and sure enough, the pretty brunette Sterling called wife and lifebond stood at a lab table looking through a microscope.

"Hi Kel," she said, glancing up at him. "How is Sonia and when can I meet her?" She took one look at him and rephrased. "What's wrong?"

Kel started to pace, ignoring the question. "She has dreams that come true."

"I heard something about that. Sterling said you thought they'd gone away?"

"I did," he said. "But apparently they're back."

"For how long?"

He stopped walking and ran his hand through his hair. "We didn't exactly get to that."

"She was pretty upset over you faking your death?"

He nodded. "That's an understatement."

"I can understand her being upset."

"I had to do it."

"I know," she said gently. "If anyone knows I do. Remember? I was inside the Zodius facility. I saw what they do to women there."

"I don't want this life for her."

"She's already a part of it," Becca reminded him.

"If I wipe her memory, I need to know if the dreams will recreate them. I need you to test her and find out."

"Kel, I touch someone and I see their memories. I can't see what their future memories will be. And if she has this ability, you can wipe away her past, but you won't stop her dreams from taking her where they want to go. Call me a romantic, but I'd like to think they will always lead her right back here, to you. You love her and you hurt every day being away from her. I see it in your eyes."

"How do I bring her into this world and justify that as okay?"

"How do you justify doing what the army did to you and the others in 'Project Zodius' by denying her the ability to choose?"

"Because I'm saving her life and they were taking ours."

"You think stealing her memories and giving her some life she didn't ask for is saving her?"

"DO you know where Kel is?" came a muffled female, very familiar voice from the hallway.

That she'd come hunting for him shouldn't have surprised him, yet it did. She was, and always had been, determined to get what she wanted. That she wanted him both warmed him and turned him to ice. He didn't know how to handle this right. He'd had no time to think about this.

Becca smiled. "She's looking for you. I like her already."

Suddenly, the door opened behind Kel and Damion said, "You have company." Kel turned just in time to see Damion step out of the doorway and Sonia appear from behind him.

"Kel," she said, charging forward to embrace him, tilting her chin up to find his eyes with hers. "All that matters is that you're alive and we're together. I love you. I never stopped loving you, or missing you, or hurting from the loss of you. I'm not letting you play macho super soldier and send me away. Not unless you tell me you don't love me anymore."

Kel buried his head in her hair, inhaling the sweet smell of woman - his woman - and he knew why he'd walked away without giving her a choice. She was a giving, beautiful woman in so many ways. She was at that bar tonight to save the waitress, fearless for herself. "I don't want to hurt you."

She pulled back and forced him to look at her, those gorgeous green eyes of hers seeming to see right into his soul, her voice hoarse with emotion. "Then don't leave me again."

"I don't want to," he assured her, and there was no way she could possibly know how much he meant those words, how much he wanted to be selfish and keep her with him.

"But you're going to?" she challenged, seeming to read his mind. She shook her head. "No. I won't let you." There was stubbornness, passion, and love, in that vow.

It was all he could do not to pick up Sonia and carry her out of here, back to the apartments he called his own when in the city. To his bed. Somehow, he managed to restrain himself and instead he gently took her hand. "Let's go back to the room."

She nodded and he turned to Becca. "Sonia, this is Becca. I'll introduce you more formally later."

Sonia waved. "Hi, Becca. Nice to meet you."

Becca smiled softly. "We'll get acquainted after you two get some much needed time together. I'd love to hear about your dreams. I have a few abilities of my own I'm still getting used to."

"I'd like that very much," Sonia said.

Kel motioned to the door and he and Sonia headed to the hallway. The floral scent of her, the soft sway of her hips, seeped into his senses.

Suddenly, his adrenaline was pumping fiercely, his blood burning through his veins. He been so long without her, too long without her. But there were things she had to know, things about him, and he dreaded the moment she might call him a monster. The moment she saw what he'd really become. And he was afraid that moment was now.

CHAPTER FIVE

The minute they were in the hallway, Kel fought the urge to pick Sonia up, as something primitive and wholly male inside him began to expand and take control. They walked past rows of apartments, adrenaline pumping through him with every step, every long second. The instant they were inside the apartment and he shut the door, the adrenaline pouring through him surged and took over. This time he really did pick her up and carried her to the bed, going down onto the mattress with her on her back, the soft and delicate curves of her body beneath his bigger, harder form.

He kissed her, driven by passion, by a wild, almost desperate need to claim her. His hands slid over her body, over her breasts. She moaned softly into his mouth and fire burned inside him, and he knew he was millimeters from forgetting everything but this moment, forgetting the consequences.

He tore his mouth from hers, his words gravely with desire. "There are things you need to know."

"I know the most important part. You're alive."

"I'm not human, Sonia. Not anymore."

"You're still the man I love."

"You don't know-"

"I know you."

"I've changed."

"Show me," she whispered. "Show me who you are now."

He kissed her, a deep passionate kiss that bled like lifeblood into him, powerful, passionate, yet oh so sweet. But he didn't want sweet. He wanted the heat, the fierceness of what they felt when they were together, what he'd been without for so very long.

Kel deepened the kiss, drinking her in, thirsting for her as he had never thirsted. He wanted the lifebond mark that would show on her neck if they bonded to appear, knowing that it would, because lifebonds weren't created from science, but from love. It was the one thing they knew of the bond, and the one thing he knew existed between him and Sonia. He craved that bond, justifying his actions, even as he swore he would not bond with her. As long as he didn't exchange blood she would not be bound to him in life and death. But if he was forced to erase her memories, some part of him would stay with her with that marking.

He touched her, everywhere and anywhere. She clung to him, arched against him, responding with such utter passion that there was no way she wasn't his lifebond. No way he could stop needing, and wanting, and caressing. His lips caressed her neck, and she tilted her head, giving him more, but not enough. Never enough. There was too much time to make up for, too many ways he wanted to know her again. Too much possibility that this was it, all he would ever have of her. "You're beautiful," he whispered in her ear, before he was kissing her again, ravenous with need. "You have no idea how much I missed you."

"I know how empty I was without you," she said, her breath heavy, her voice a whisper. There was real pain beneath those words that hurt him. Without the ability to wipe away memories he had now, he'd hurt her.

He kissed her again, desperate to make her forget the pain, to give her pleasure. His mouth trailed downward, over her breasts, and he pushed her shirt upward, removing the barriers between them. They'd had too many of those. They still did. She quickly rid herself of her sweatshirt and tank top. Impatient to see her, to feel her, he unhooked her bra while her arms were still over her head, filling his hands with her naked breasts before she'd even tossed away the garment.

He lapped at her nipples, suckling and licking, knowing how it turned her on. He knew her. He knew what she liked. The thought that some other man might know almost destroyed him. It's why he'd had Sterling watching out for her, why he never asked if she was dating. He had no right to know, to ask. He'd lost her.

The thought was lost to the gentle twine of her fingers into his hair, the way her back arched forward, and the soft little purring sounds coming from her mouth. He missed those sounds more than he'd realized. He missed every inch of her and he set out to kiss every spot he should have been kissing for the past few years.

Kel barely remembered undressing, or how her pants and shoes came off. Impatiently, he ripped the tiny piece of black lace panties she wore away, removing everything that separated her from him. He was hot and hard, and he burned wickedly to be inside her, to feel her tight around him. To claim her as his again.

But he wanted this memory to last, he wanted it to be powerful enough to become her dreams, to defeat his power to erase her memories. It was a ridiculous thought, and an impossible idea, but it was the one that drove him, pushed him, made him have the power to pull back, to go slow when he wanted everything she was and ever would be now.

His hands were all over her body, her soft skin like a drug. He kissed her stomach, caressing her hips with his palms and then trailing his lips over the curve of one of them, traveling a path down her thigh and then back up.

Tension coiled in her body beneath his hands and mouth. He could feel her stomach quiver under his palm where he rested it.

By the time his slid his shoulders between her legs and stroked the slick wet heat of her body with his tongue, they were both on edge, both shaking with need. He lapped at her, the salty feminine taste of her seeping into his senses, driving him wild. Somehow, he restrained himself, going slowly, licking and suckling as he slid two fingers inside her until she was on edge. Until she wanted harder and faster and he gave it to her, his reward being her gasp and then the spasm of her body around his fingers. Then she did what she always did. She turned her head and hid her face, embarrassed by the intensity of her orgasm. God, he loved that side of her, the woman who could be so vulnerable no matter how many times or ways, they made love.

He slid up her body, pulled her mouth to his and kissed her. Her shyness slipped away as they faced each other. Her gaze slid over the tattoo of angel wings on his left shoulder and arm. He'd gotten them when he was in a dark moment, in need of some faith.

Her beautiful green eyes lifted to his, filled with mischief. "Sexy. I like."

"Do you now?" he asked, his blood heating as he pulled her on top of him and repeated her earlier words. "Show me."

She smiled and kissed him, reaching behind her to stroke his cock and shifting to guide him inside her. The instant he felt the wet heat of her body, his lashes lowered, sensations roaring through him as she took him fully.

Together they sighed in pleasure and relief. "I love you," he whispered, threading his fingers in the soft honey-colored strands of her hair. "I love you so much, Sonia. I was only trying to protect you."

"Don't protect me like that again," she ordered.

He couldn't promise that, and he didn't promise that. He kissed her instead, thrusting into her at the same time, losing the question to the heat, the burn, the joining of their bodies. A slow sensual rhythm emerged, the two of them moving as one, kissing and swaying.

Sonia lifted her upper body away from him, sitting up to ride him, and he held her hips as she started to move, watched as her gaze swept his body and settled on one of the many tattoos he'd gotten in the past two years.

She stopped moving, her hand sweeping over the design. "You had my name tattooed on your chest?"

He gently pulled her to him, holding her close. "Because if this day ever came I didn't want you to have any doubt you were always on my mind."

She made a soft sound of surprise. "I love you," she whispered and pressed her lips to his. He parted her lips, and tasted the salt of her tears, the emotion they represented. The slow raw need between them turned to wild, hot passion. They exploded in a frenzy of touching and thrusting until they were shaking again, this time with release. And when he held her in his arms, expecting the burn of the mating mark to cause her to react and she didn't, he understood her tears, understood what she feared. That this was the end not the beginning. She wasn't his lifebond. It was the one thing in the back of his mind that he now knew he hadn't wanted to discover, but he had to know. She was destined for someone else. He had to set her free and it was going to destroy him.

KEL

CHAPTER SIX

Sonia lay beside Kel, her head to his chest, the soft rhythm of his heart music to her ears. "Tell me about your dreams," he said, stroking her hair. "When did they come back?"

Her mind tracked back to the torment of the past few years, of losing him, of what followed. Awake and asleep she'd been in hell.

"They started about a year after you left, and they got...more graphic. I saw people die. I saw the blood. I felt pain and fear that was theirs but felt like mine. I wanted an escape and I didn't want to know they were real. I stopped watching the news or reading the internet and papers. I went to the doctor. She told me it was from the trauma of losing you and gave me pills."

"What?" he asked, shifting her so that they were side by side, still on top of the blankets they'd never pulled down. "They drugged you?"

"I was desperate," she argued. "I dreamed of a young girl in a car accident. I was in a store and they had the televisions on and I saw the news. It was her, but Kel she'd died the night before. I couldn't have stopped it, or that's what I believed at the time because she was dead when I woke up. I was hysterical, and even my faith was tested. You were dead. I was seeing other people die and I couldn't stop it. I needed help and this doctor, a dream specialist, said I was using real life to build my dreams."

"She convinced you that you somehow saw these stories and then recreated them in your dreams?"

"That's right and at first, Kel, I thought she was right. The medicine stopped the dreams and I was okay. Only I wasn't. The dreams came back and more powerfully. They adjusted my meds. They came back again. Finally, I said no more."

She watched relief wash over his face. "Good. You don't need medicine. You just need to learn how to deal with the dreams. If anyone has learned that unique abilities are possible, it's me and there are people here who can help you do that." Regret etched his brow. "We could have helped you long before now. I made so many wrong choices with you, Sonia. I'm so sorry."

She kissed him. "You were trying to protect me. Don't do it again, but I know that. Besides, I did a lot of research and decided to stop fighting the dreams. I began writing a journal of all I remembered the minute I woke up. It took a year, but I finally realized that I dreamed about the people involved in the accidents for weeks but only remembering the tragic events because they woke me up. Still, I didn't know how to find the people and help them. Until recently, that is. Now, I can pick up landmarks and hone in on the places and people. I'm getting better and better at it. I even see flashes of the dreams when I'm awake. It's what I'm meant to do, Kel. I'm supposed to save these people." She held her fist to her chest."I feel it in my very soul."

"It's dangerous," he said. "You can't go playing cop when you aren't one."

"I applied for the FBI," she said. "I'm close to getting in. I should have stayed on that path in the first place." A sudden pain ripped down her spine and then blasted into her neck. "Oh god." She sat up and held her nape. "Ah. Ouch. Something is biting me, Kel." She turned around and grabbed her hair, feeling panic rise inside her. "Get it off. Get it off my neck."

He brushed aside her hair and kissed her neck, then tried to pull her against his body.

"Kel!" she shouted. "Stop. Get it off. What is it?" she demanded, rotating to face him and shoving her hair out of her eyes. She was appalled to discover he was smiling. "You're smiling at my pain?"

"No, I-"

"You're grinning now!" She scooted off the bed away from him. "I can't believe you would laugh at this. It hurts." Only, the pain was fading and she barely felt anything now. Still – he was smiling. Her gaze found the bathroom and she ran for it, uncaring of her nudity. Kel knew her body. He was about to know her wrath, too.

She used the mirror of the medicine cabinet beside the sink to try and see her neck, but she couldn't get her hair out of the way. Kel appeared in front of her, looking sexy as sin, and damn him for making her notice. She was furious with him, even though the pain was completely gone.

He framed her body with his and there was no missing returned arousal, but as her gaze lifted she gasped, the now absent pain in her neck, forgotten.

"Your eyes are black. Oh God. So very black. What's wrong? Were you bitten too?"

His lips curved, those dark eyes dancing with mischief. "It's part of the GTECH change."

"Why are you smiling again?"

"I'm not. Okay, maybe I am. I'll explain after you look at your neck." He lifted her hair. It took her a moment to tear her gaze from the deep, dark depths of his stare, only to gasp again at what she found in the mirror.

She touched the double circle etched into her skin with a intricate woven design around the edges, as if someone had taken great time and caution to tattoo her. "How is this possible? Was it when I was passed out?"

"No. I wouldn't let that happen." He framed her face with his hands. "It's a lifebond circle. GTECHs are another race, Sonia. We are faster and stronger than humans. We are immune to human illness. We do not age and we heal rapidly. Some of us have other abilities as well. And we can only reproduce with one female, in one season of the year. If the two people are meant to bond, it happens after the first act of sex."

He was speaking another language, making no sense. Or she was dreaming and kept convincing herself she wasn't. "This isn't our first time having sex, though."

"It's the first time since I fully transitioned," he said. "The lifebonding process didn't develop until we began to evolve as GTECHs. And by the way, I can mask the color of my eyes to anyone but you, my lifebond."

She was stunned and confused. All this talk of GTECHs felt unreal, but yet he wasn't. Kel not only felt very real but being with him made her feel complete in a way she'd never thought she would again. "Lifebond," she repeated, trying to get her mind around the word and the idea it represented.

"A biological mating," he explained. "Marriage of the bodies. And that's why I was smiling when your neck hurt, because I knew what it was." He lowered his head, brushing his lips over hers. "It means you belong to me and I belong to you and nothing but death can take that from us. And now, unless you have a problem with it, I'm going to make love to my lifebond."

There was something she could understand and embrace and embrace it she would.

A long time later, Sonia collapsed on the mattress beside Kel, sated and happier than she had been in a very long time. He lay on his back beside her and they both stared up at the ceiling in a comfortable, wonderful silence until her thoughts found a voice.

"So do the GTECHs work for the Army?"

"No," he said. "The Army tried to kill off and destroy their mistake, meaning us."

She rolled over to look at him and found him staring at her. "You've got to be kidding me."

"I wish I was," he said. "We've made a truce of sorts. We're all working to stop the Zodius from gaining more power, but they'd slit our throats in a heartbeat."

"So this operation you have is completely private?"

"It is," he said. "A couple of the men, Damion included, come from filthy rich families and we have enough private donations to make up what they can't."

She rolled back over and thought about that. "This is all so incredible." She eased to her side again with another thought. "I don't really understand wind walking or GTECHs or much of anything you've told me, just so you know."

"Neither do I," he laughed, "and I've been living it for years now."

"So you travel in the wind how?"

"It's like becoming the wind," he said. "No physical presence but complete awareness."

"Can I wind walk with you?"

"Humans can't wind walk without the risk of death."

"Oh, well then," she said. "That doesn't sound so intriguing anymore. Wind walking sounds impossible."

"So does someone dreaming about the future." He ran his hand over her hair. "You should sleep. I'll take you to see Sunrise City tomorrow and you'll be able to answer all of your questions there."

"Sunrise City?"

"It's the Renegades' underground headquarters," he said. "And when I say city, I mean city. We have restaurants and stores, and about anything a normal city would have. Our population is nearly a thousand now. Only a few hundred of those are GTECHs. The rest are humans helping to fight the Zodius or women rescued from Adam's testing facilities."

Her brows furrowed. "Why would you take them there?"

"There are GTECHs that we call 'trackers' who can locate certain people if they aren't beneath the ground."

"Certain people as in who?"

"A GTECH who doesn't have his mental shield up. That only happens when we're injured. Or," he hesitated, "this is where the grim part of this war comes into play."

"Tell me," she urged.

"Any women who has had sex with a GTECH can be tracked by another GTECH. It creates a different kind of energy. It's impossible to explain."

Her eye went wide. "Meaning me?"

"No," he said. "I'd never put you in danger like that. You are my lifebond and I have the ability to shield you. Again, it's hard to explain, but I can shield you just as I do myself."

"You didn't know I was your lifebond."

"Yes," he said with absoluteness, pulling her close and kissing her. "I did."

"You said it's rare."

"So are we." He brushed his lips over hers. "There are things you need to know, about me, and about our bond. But you need rest. We have a good two-hour drive tomorrow." He kissed her forehead. "So sleep before I don't let you."

She smiled and caressed his cheek. "What about you?"

"GTECHs don't need much sleep, but I'll be right here with you. I'm not going anywhere."

She wanted to believe that more than she'd ever wanted to believe anything, but she sensed there was something he wasn't telling her. Something she feared but she wasn't going to think about it now. She curled up to him, letting the warmth of his body seep into hers and she let herself dream that this would be the first night of the rest of their lives together.

KEL

CHAPTER SEVEN

Sonia woke the next morning to the sound of Kel humming nearby and the smell of coffee and this time it was her turn to smile. She stretched and sat up, holding the sheet to her chest.

"Morning," he said, from over at the bar, a spoon in his hand. "Hungry?"

"Starving," she said eagerly.

"Becca brought you some of her clothes," he said. "And a robe. It's there on the end of the bed."

Sonia reached for the pink silk garment and shoved her arms in it. A quick trip to the bathroom and she was at the kitchen table, being rewarded with a kiss from a sexy, bare-chested super soldier, and being ordered to sit at the table.

"Fine." She laughed. "But for the record, a girl could get used to being waited on hand and spatula by a hot soldier."

"As long as that soldier is me," he said with a grin. "I don't have a problem with that. Give me about one minute and my famous omelet will be served up."

"I can't wait she said, watching him fill her plate before returning and setting it in front of her.

"Brunch is served," he said. "I haven't made one since I, well, died, so I don't promise it's as good as the past."

Since he died. That was a bad memory she could do without. "I'm sure it's great. Thank you." She was just about to take a bite when he returned with two more plates. "Is someone joining us?"

He sat down with her. "Nope. GTECHs eat a lot. It's our metabolism." He poured orange juice into his glass. "And we have a vitamin C deficiency. Our scientific teams are trying to figure it out." He poured her some juice as well.

"So you mentioned special abilities that certain GTECHs have?" she asked, tearing into her omelet. "What exactly does that mean?"

"Caleb can sense emotions and I'm not sure he can't read minds. He hasn't said as much, but I've got my suspicions. Michael, who I don't think you have met, can control and communicate with the wind in some freaky way none of us understand."

"But you travel in the wind."

"He commands the wind. I'm talking throw a wind ball or use it as a wall. Crazy stuff." He considered a moment. "Sterling doesn't have anything unique, but his wife Becca is one of the most powerful people among us. She was given a synthetic dose of the GTECH serum in one of Adam's fertility camps. She's telepathic and she sees the past of the person she touches. Oh yeah, and she can command a GTECH to sleep and they go lights out better than with a switch. She's a weapon, times ten."

She gaped, not sure which part shocked her the most. "Becca was captured by Adam?"

He nodded. "So were a lot of the women at Sunrise City. They operate a task force to track down areas where women are being abducted and stop it. But only Becca has those skills. Caleb said, like you, she had some natural-born skills that came out with the serum. As for the other GTECHs, over time, different skills emerge. We seem to be evolving."

"Wow," she said, sitting back in her chair. "Just wow."

"It's a lot to take in," he said. "Sometimes I feel like I'm dreaming. But as you can see, feeling awkward about your dreaming and visions isn't an issue here. In fact, I have a feeling that between Becca and Caleb, you can learn to harness your ability even more than you have on your own. Caleb did a lot to help Becca."

"That would be remarkable," she said. "To have people who understand and help me rather than call me crazy. It's almost too good to be true."

He studied her a long moment before shoving his plate aside and going down on his knees beside her. He turned her chair so that he braced both hands on the arm. "This world exists because we are in a war. I need you to know that. And I need you to understand that Adam is hunting you. You can't go back to your old life. It kills me to think of you wrapped up in this hell almost as badly as it kills me to think of you not being here."

Emotion tightened in her chest, and her hand covered his. She was remarkably calm, and a sense of rightness filled her. "I let my dreams scare me away from my purpose, which I believe is to protect and help people. You can't scare me away any more than they can now. I'm going to put my dreams to use, and it seems to me that dreaming of the women being kidnapped means I belong in this war."

He considered her another long moment. "I'll be overly protective."

"I'll make you get over it."

"Adam Rain is hunting you."

"You've already made that clear."

"You can't go back to your life. You can't even go home and get your things. I'll get them for you."

That was hard to swallow but she wasn't foolish enough to take risks. She'd seen too much in her dreams to not believe in real life nightmares. "I understand."

His lips thinned. "No. You don't. Not this world or this war. Not yet. But you will and when you do I need you to know that you aren't stuck here with me. We can move you somewhere, get you a new identity-"

She leaned down and kissed him. "I belong in this war, fighting by your side."

He wrapped his arm around her and pulled her off the chair, his head pressed to her stomach, holding her a long moment before he looked up at her. "I want you by my side and I feel like such a selfish bastard for that."

Her fingers traced the soft strands of his light brown hair. "Say you're sorry when you eat the last piece of chocolate in the box," she teased, remembering their mutual love of candy. "Don't be sorry for wanting me by your side." And with that, he pulled her down onto the ground and they forgot about breakfast until well after lunch.

A few hours later, Sonia sat in the lab with Becca, who Sonia liked more every second she was with her. A safe location for Carrie, the waitress from the bar, had been found and the trip to Sunrise had to be put off a day to get her settled. Sonia felt such satisfaction to know that she'd saved Carrie, though she hated that Kel felt Carrie was now a target for Adam. Carrie, like herself, had to move and leave her life behind.

Sonia indicated the pink tee she wore with Becca's dark blue jeans that luckily fit fairly well, and laughed, "'Astrobiologists have more fun'?"

Becca grinned. "And you thought it was blondes."

Sonia laughed. "Sterling is blonde."

"And I bought him a shirt that says 'Blondes have more fun' and he said he'd only wear it if he could add 'in bed'."

Sonia almost choked on the soda she was sipping. "Oh my God. That's too funny." She set her drink aside, deciding it was dangerous for now. "I don't think I've ever known an astrobiologist or anyone else who has."

"It's an interest in space and other forms of life that got many in my field killed or kidnapped by Adam. It's a long story." Her brows furrowed. "I wonder...I can see a person's past when I touch them. So if I touch you, I'm curious if your dreams would read like your past. Because if they do, then maybe we can harness that to better hone in on female targets and save would be victims."

Excitement rose inside Sonia. "Oh, let's try!"

The door to the lab opened and a tall, extremely good-looking man with longish brown hair, wearing a whole lot of leather, sauntered in. "Where's the Eraser? Calling the Eraser." He stopped dead when he saw Sonia. "Oh, sorry about that. You must be Sonia." He offered her his hand and she took it, before he added. "I'm Chale, Kel's friend, and Damion's frenemey."

"Frenemey?" she asked, finding she was smiling far more than one would expect having just been thrown into the Twilight Zone.

"He hates me so much he likes me. So where is the Eraser?" He eyed Sonia. "Our team is a few miles from Carrie's new location and they need Kel to wind walk over and work his magic on arrival."

"Eraser?" Sonia asked, confused.

"That's what we call Kel since he can erase people's memories."

Sonia went completely still.

"Sonia don't overreact," Becca said quickly. "He would have told you. He hasn't had time."

"Oh shit," Chale said. "You didn't know, did you?"

"No," Kel said from the door. "She didn't know because I didn't have time to tell her, so thank you for that."

Sonia was on her feet in a heartbeat. "You had time to tell me, you just didn't. You were going to wipe my memories and send me away again, weren't you?"

CHAPTER EIGHT

You were going to wipe my memories and send me away again, weren't you?

Kel's heart thundered in his chest as he replayed Sonia's words and tried to figure out what to say and not say. "I wasn't going to erase your memories. Or I was. I thought about it. I was going to give you the choice if you hated Sunrise City or this life. A choice, Sonia."

"Then why not tell me?" she demanded.

"I did at breakfast."

"You said nothing about wiping my memories."

"I knew you'd react like this."

"Are you wiping Carrie's memories, too?" she demanded.

"We have no choice," he said. "It's that or a life in Sunrise City."

Sterling walked into the room and stopped next to Kel. His gaze slid around the room before he muttered one of his famously outlandish statements turning Holy Mother of God into, "Holy M&Ms we're fighting, aren't we?"

"Yes," Sonia said at the same time Kel said, "No."

"So yes," Sterling said and glanced at Kel. "Sorry, man. Her face says it all. And I hate to make this worse, but we have a team ready to follow us to Carrie's new location. We need to get a move on."

Kel ran his hand through his hair. "I'd planned to talk to you about this before we left for Sunrise today. I had no idea they would find her a location as quickly as they did. Can we talk a minute, Sonia?"

"Go take care of Carrie," she said, shaking her head. "This isn't something we're going to solve while other people wait."

Damn it, he'd say this with an audience if he had to. He crossed the room, grabbed her and kissed her. "You are everything to me. The thought of going one more second, let alone the rest of my life without you, shreds me to pieces. And yes, I considered wiping your memory, I won't lie. I admit it. I wanted to protect you and I won't apologize for that. I love you and I wanted you to have a choice, after you saw the real picture of what you're involved with. But know this. I believe you're right about the dreams leading you here and to a purpose. We're supposed to fight this war together. I'll be back in two hours tops."

He kissed her again and turned and strode out of the room. The hours away from her were going to be torture.

"It's a soldier and a GTECHs nature to protect people, but their women even more so," Becca said when she and Sonia were finally alone.

Sonia absorbed her words and tried to calm down, sinking back onto a stool. "I know, but he let me think he was dead."

"He had a reason," she said. "If the Army didn't grab you and call you a witness and turn you into a casualty to protect a secret, Adam would have gotten to you. I was inside Area 51 and I know what they would have done to you just because you're his woman. Every man in that place would have tried to mate with you and then they would have used drugs and tried it again. He didn't know if he would have the power to protect you from that back then."

Sonia inhaled and slowly let out her breath as she confessed, "It hurt."

"I know," Becca said. "But he hurt just like you. I see how different he is in just the short time you've been here. Give him a chance. He needs you here. He knows that." She smiled. "We all need you. You have amazing abilities."

Sonia felt the tension drain from her body. "You're right. I overreacted." They talked a while and then played around with mixing their abilities with remarkable success. Becca was picking up on her dreams.

Three hours had passed, and Sonia felt a gnawing worry in her stomach. She told herself it was simply that she hated fighting with Kel, that she was in emotional knots, but deep down it felt like more. "Shouldn't they be back?"

"Things can drag out on missions," she said. "Why don't we take you on a tour of the building so you know your way around."

Thirty minutes later, Sonia was in her room, promising to take a nap to be alert when Kel returned, but she just couldn't shake the bad feeling inside. Another half hour and she went in search of answers.

She ended up beside a computer room, when she overheard Sterling saying, "They've been out of communication too long."

"I'm the best tracker we have," Damion said. "I'll go check things out. If anyone's down, I'll know."

She hurried into the room. "You're talking about Kel and Carrie, aren't you?" Damion and Sterling exchanged a look and she said, "That's a 'yes'. How long have they been out of contact?"

47

"They're fine," Damion said. "They're traveling through an area with limited cell coverage. We know that. We just like to be cautious."

"Are you going to check on them?" she asked Damion.

"Yes. I'll go now." He walked towards her and paused. "He'll be fine. He is fine."

"Please be right." She'd lost him once. She couldn't lose him again.

"I am," he said and headed towards the door she now knew was a tunnel to a warehouse they used to wind walk out of sight.

"I'll come and get you when I know something," Sterling offered. "Or I can send Becca down to keep you company?"

She shook her head. "No, thanks. I'm fine." But she wasn't. She headed back down the hallway when something about the words triggered a sudden flash of images in her mind. Kel and several other Renegades being attacked on the highway. The images blurred together but she saw Kel grab Carrie and throw her on the ground, just in time to take a blast of bullets. She gasped and started running for the door.

She was down the ramp and screaming after Damion, a vague memory of dream in her mind, of Kel needing her. "He's down," she yelled. "He's hurt. They're all hurt."

Damion turned and met her halfway. "How do you know?"

"I saw it. I can see things I can't explain. Not now. I'm going with you. I can read the landmarks from my vision."

Damion held up his hands. "Oh no. That's not happening. You can't wind walk unless you've lifebonded."

"I have," she said, wondering why Kel hadn't told her that but not caring. Not right now. "We did. You can check my neck."

"Sonia, then you can relax," he said. "Once you do the blood bond, and convert to GTECH, if he dies, you die. If he's mortally hurt it would bring you to your knees. Let him focus on keeping you both alive. Let me go so I can come back and tell you he's safe. And he's darn sure going to want to be the first one to take you on a wind walk."

"Blood bond?" she asked, feeling sick. Kel hadn't completed the lifebond process with her. He had been going to wipe her memory. She drew in a breath and forced it out. It didn't matter. He was dying. She knew it and she had to save him. Even if they said goodbye later. She buried her face in her hands like she was crying and rushed at Damion, pretending to hug him but took his gun instead.

She backed up and pointed it at him. "I'm going with you."

"Oh, well hell," he grumbled, running his hand through his light brown hair, a scowl on his too handsome face. "You really know how to wound a guy's pride. Can we make a deal and not tell anyone about this?"

"Just take me with you."

"Shoot me, Sonia. I don't care. But I'm not taking you on a walk that could kill you."

"You have to!" She shouted, she didn't know why, but she felt it in her core, that she was the difference in Kel living or dying. "Please. Trust me on this. He needs me right now."

"He needs you," he agreed softly, his hazel eyes filled with understanding. "That's my point, Sonia. I can't let anything happen to you. I won't let anything happen to you."

There were shouts down the tunnel and Sonia couldn't believe her eyes. Chale was running with Kel thrown over his shoulder.

"Call the doc," Chale shouted. "They had Green Hornets."

"What are Green Hornets?" Sonia asked, rushing towards them.

Damion was already reaching for his phone even as he asked Chale, "Where's Carrie?"

Chale glanced at Sonia. "He'll be okay. We heal quickly and then to Damion, "She's underground and we have a team getting her to Sunrise."

The rest was a blur for Sonia. She barely remembered how she ended up in a hospital-like room, standing back as several people she didn't know and Becca ripped open some kind of special second skin bulletproof vest that Kel wore and she surmised that Green Hornets were bullets. There was blood. So much blood. Too much blood. Tears streamed down her face, fear and helplessness welling inside her. Then they were operating, right there, without any special tools, just pulling out bullet after bullet.

"Oh God," she whispered. "This is going to kill him."

"Come here, Sonia," Becca called out from the bedside, holding a towel over one of the bleeding wounds. Oh God. There were so many holes. Becca pointed to a monitor where a pretty blonde female was displayed on the screen.

"Sonia, I'm Kelly," she said. "I'm the Chief of Medical Staff for the Renegades. Listen, honey, we don't have long here. I understand you're his lifebond."

"Yes," Sonia managed.

"Okay, good. But you haven't done the blood exchange?"

She shook her head. "No."

"Okay. GTECHs can survive most injuries but there is something called a healing sickness. It's caused by the vitamin C deficiency. When the injuries are too extreme, it's intense. The more advance the GTECH in his special abilities, the more it seems to affect him. There's something I've been experimenting with to try to combat it. The bullets are out so he has the ability to heal if we can trigger the reaction. I need you to do the blood exchange now. If my initial testing is right, it will overcome the vitamin C deficiency."

A dream took vivid form in Sonia's mind, a dream of this moment, and she now knew why she'd been so irrationally desperate to get Damion to take her with him. "Yes, okay. Anything to save him."

"Sonia," Kelly said. "Once you do this-"

"I die if he dies," she supplied, "and that means now, today. I understand. I'll do it. Of course, I'll do it. Just save him. Please. Save him."

Kel woke in his bed, the scent of her around him, the soft strands of her honey-colored hair caressing his skin while her soft fingers traced the angel wing on his arm. The last thing he remembered were the bullets, the pain, and the darkness, but now, the wounds were gone.

"Since I'm naked and you're not," he murmured, "I'm assuming I didn't miss anything I didn't want to."

She laughed. "No, but your clothes were bloody and every time I tried to dress you, you rolled over."

"My own personal angel caring for me," he said. "I'm really dead this time and you're the dream, aren't I?" he asked softly, capturing her hand with his and sucking in a breath when their gazes locked. "Your eyes-"

"Are black," she supplied. "Yes. They are. Because you see, us GTECH women only have one man and-"

He pulled her to him and kissed her, happier than he thought he'd ever been. "We did the blood exchange?"

"Yes," she said. "The doc said it would save your life."

Realization washed over him like ice water. "So you had to do it."

"I was going to say the same thing," she argued. "You had to do it. You didn't tell me about it so maybe you didn't want to be stuck with me forever and ever."

He smiled and rolled her to her back, settling on top of her. "For your information I had planned the blood exchange for a very special moment." He kissed her and rolled over, reaching to the bedside table before turning back so that they lay facing each other. "I went and picked this up from your house today." He set the velvet box between them and opened the lid to display the white diamond ring he'd given her years before. "I planned to ask you to marry me again when I knew this world was where you wanted to be. And then, we'd do the blood exchange. We are bound by blood, but we don't have to live together. It's still a choice. So I'm asking you to make that choice now. Marry me, Sonia. Spend forever with me and I promise I will make up the past few years to you."

She studied him a long moment. "When would you have decided to ask me? When would I have been a part of your world?"

"The minute I knew you saw how brutal it was, and you still said you wanted to be here. I'd say you know. So, Sonia—"

"Yes," she said, wrapping her arms around him and pressing close to him. "Yes. I will marry you, and no, you don't have to make anything up to me. Just love me, Kel. Just love me."

"That's the easiest thing anyone has ever asked me to do. Because I do. I love you, Sonia, more than I knew anyone could love."

THE END

Don't miss the rest of the Zodius series available now!
Michael
Sterling
Kel
Damion

KEL

Also by Lisa Renee Jones

The Inside Out Series

If I Were You
Being Me
Revealing Us
His Secrets*
Rebecca's Lost Journals
The Master Undone*
My Hunger*
No In Between
My Control*
I Belong to You
All of Me*

The Secret Life of Amy Bensen

Escaping Reality
Infinite Possibilities
Forsaken
Unbroken*

Careless Whispers

Denial
Demand
Surrender

Dirty Money

Hard Rules
Damage Control
Bad Deeds
End Game
White Lies
Provocative
Shameless

Lilah Love

Murder Notes
Murder Girl (July 2018)

*eBook only

ABOUT THE AUTHOR

New York Times and *USA Today* bestselling author Lisa Renee Jones is the author of the highly acclaimed INSIDE OUT series. Suzanne Todd (producer of *Alice in Wonderland*) on the INSIDE OUT series: *Lisa has created a beautiful, complicated, and sensual world that is filled with intrigue and suspense. Sara's character is strong, flawed, complex, and sexy - a modern girl we all can identify with.*

In addition to the success of Lisa's INSIDE OUT series, she has published many successful titles. The TALL, DARK AND DEADLY series and THE SECRET LIFE OF AMY BENSEN series, both spent several months on a combination of the New York Times and USA Today bestselling lists. Lisa is also the author of the bestselling DIRTY MONEY and WHITE LIES series. Presently, Lisa is working on her Murder Girl/Lilah Love series to be published by Montlake.

Prior to publishing Lisa owned multi-state staffing agency that was recognized many times by The Austin Business Journal and also praised by the Dallas Women's Magazine. In 1998 Lisa was listed as the #7 growing women owned business in Entrepreneur Magazine.

Lisa loves to hear from her readers. You can reach her at www.lisareneejones.com and she is active on Twitter and Facebook daily.

Printed in Great Britain
by Amazon